ANDROMEDA GALAXY

Number of moons: 6

Number of moons: 2

Number of moons: 1

of moons: 1

Lembak-Krokur

moons: 12

HROOF

Orbitum Lembak-Krokur 176 million kilometers

Orbitum Maximum Shambok 1,875 million kilometers

Gish

Shambok

Shivik

Orbitum Maximum Shivik 5,589 million kilometers; moons: 1

In orbit around Gas Giant; Orbitum Maximum Arboreon 216 million kilometers; moons: 7

Arboreon

Orbitum Maximum Torper 107 million kilometers

Orbitum Maximum Ploploplop 15 million kilometers

Torper

moons: 4

Ploploplop

moons: none

ZUMA

DONATO 2007

1 January 2500

Greetings, Earthlings.

Astron here. My mother unit is Longwon, ambassador from the planet Dasu in the Tri-Star Republic of the Andromeda Galaxy. Mom has asked me to tell you all about the Republic in this book.

I go *wagwag* over space travel, and I know you will, too. I can't wait to show you some of my favorite places in the three solar systems of our Tri-Star Republic. They may be alien worlds to you, but they're home to me. I promise you a fascinating trip.

Astron

FLOOR
348

ipicturebooks.com
24 W. 25th St.
New York, NY 10010

Visit us at http://www.ipicturebooks.com All rights reserved. Text copyright © 2002 by ipicturebooks.com Illustrations copyright © 2002 by Donato Giancola

Book design by Rosanne Kakos-Main

ISBN 1-59019-929-4
LCCN 2001099870

MON
Printed in Spain

VISIT MY ALIEN WORLDS

BY
DONATO GIANCOLA

WITH TEXT BY
MARC GAVE

ipicturebooks
New York
www.ipicturebooks.com
Distributed by Little, Brown and Company

What Should You Pack?

For your trip to the Republic and hops between planets, you need a superprotective, all-purpose space suit. The UPSB (Universal Protection Standards Board) makes sure that all suits meet safety standards. The really *blodni* styles will eat up your allowance fast! So wait to buy a new suit on Mengrath or Shambok for the trip back. Those are the Republic's most *blodni* fashion centers. (To learn more about these and other planets, see the map key at the end.)

For stuff to wear on our "alien worlds," visit the Rmee-Nayvi chain, run by my second cousins, and you can't go wrong. They stock gravity suits for Beluchi, amazingly waterproof outfits for Torper, and even wire mesh for Krugor. The store specializes in WonderFab, the almost weightless cloth developed by Tri-Star tailors. Some of that stuff looks so heavy. But you'll be surprised—it's actually as light as the feathers of your birds!

How Can You Get There?

TGIF (Trans-Galaxy Interplanetary Flights) has the best space-craft, hands down. I know, because Mom travels with them all the time. Each sleek ship holds 100 passengers and 20 crew members. At the highest warp speed, it takes only three days to get to the Republic.

That may sound like a long time, but don't worry. You won't be asking the crew, "Are we there yet?" There's plenty to see. Look out the windows while passing Saturn, and you might catch a glimpse of the asteroid miners working nearby. If it's your first space flight, you'll get weightless walking lessons. You'll get no-gravity eating lessons. Make sure you pay close attention to the instructions for going to the bathroom!

How Can You Stay Safe?

All TGIF craft come with comet and meteor deflectors, in addition to special shield protection against harmful space rays. Pilots stay safe from novas and other dangers behind the specially treated glass in their cockpits.

Once you arrive in the Republic, you will be allowed only on planets that are safe for humans. Even so you will need to take extra steps to avoid harm. For example, even if you're going to Lembak-Krokur, you should use sunblock you purchase on Shambok or Mengrath—SPF 145. That's *much* higher than anything sold on Earth.

What Happens When You Arrive?

Your ship will land at one of our advanced spaceports on Dasu, Arboreon, or Shambok. When Mom and I come to Earth, we often see travelers wandering around lost, but that won't happen in the spaceports of the Republic. Your flight crew will stay right by your side until you get your stuff, pass through customs, and find a ride to your hotel.

How Do You Pay For Things?

You don't carry money on Earth anymore, right? Well, you don't need any in the Republic, either. But instead of a One Earth Card, you register your handprint at customs. It becomes part of our HidenSeek (Hand Identification System Peek). The expression "Give me a hand" has an entirely new meaning in the Republic. You can do just about anything with it.

How Easy Is It to Talk?

You won't find a single phrase book on any planet in the Republic. That's because you don't need to learn any alien languages. When you land, you get your SimTrans, which you wear in your ear. It automatically translates anything anyone says into a language you understand. Simple?

Here, you can see Mom "talking" with a human space traveler and a GrowBot. Yes, the SimTrans even translates robot speech, so there's no need to learn Robot Code.

Where Can You Stay?

A deluxe suite in a 400-story hotel. A sleeping bag on a rocky crag above a valley with a river running through it. A cozy fleece-lined icehouse on the side of a vast glacier. Where do you want to stay? In the Republic, you can stay at any or all of these—and many others.

I love the view from some of our ultrahigh 400-story hotels. I go especially *wagwag* over one on Beluchi, where the whole hotel—the whole city—floats. Beds appear electronically from what look like wall panels, jets of water spray from solid-looking mirrors, kitchenettes pop up from the floor. At the clap of your hands, it's all gone from sight. You don't even need maid service!

What Kind of Food Can You Eat?

Are you afraid you won't find your favorite foods? Don't worry. In all the main cities and even some of the smaller ones, chains of Earth restaurants have opened. You can easily find a McGalaxy or a ProtoseKing. But why not try local specialties such as grilled octoplant on Arboreon, boobean burritos on Dasu, or 20-layer cake on Mengrath?

The most up-to-date eating spots have hologram menus. You just touch a button, and a 3D hologram of a food appears before you. Thanks to Smellavision, you can even smell the dish ahead of time. That cuts down a lot of "yuck" when your food comes.

What Happens If You Get Sick?

You're lucky. Travelers from Earth usually don't catch Republic germs—and our germs usually don't catch you! But too many days in low gravity, too much rich food, or an accidental collision with a huge life-form may leave you in need of some patching up. Don't worry—our doctors are the finest. As you can see, they are up on the latest techniques. And they have experience with all kinds of life-forms, even Earthlings. The best part is that your BlueMed card is good anywhere in the Republic!

The Simple Things

If you're like me, you'll get tired out from all that sightseeing, especially if you travel to different climates and gravities. So you'll just want to *frij* with some HoloGames or HoloVids. There are public arcades where you can rent your own HoloRoom for a few hours. The larger hotels have their own. And in the deluxe hotels you can get HoloGames and HoloMovies right in your room.

In the city of Pastburg on Mengrath, you can stay in hotels that imitate historical periods in different places around the galaxy. For example, you can stay in the kind of hotel that was popular around the year 2000 on Earth. You can play primitive computer games and watch VHS videotapes. I'm not kidding. If you like that retro stuff, you'll have a ball in Pastburg.

The Floating Cities of Beluchi

Another of my absolute favorite places in the Republic is Grandome, the largest of the floating cities of Beluchi. All the buildings have these walls and floors that grip your clothing, but it's fun sometimes just to float from room to room.

The Imperial Palace in Grandome is the most *hamolizent* of all the buildings. Nobody lives there anymore—it's been four centuries since any part of Beluchi has had an emperor. The palace has become a fantastic gallery for art from all over Beluchi. If you have the patience, you can get a special two-day, 137-room guided tour. But most visitors just skip that and head for the old living quarters of the emperor's family. You can even stay overnight in diamond-studded beds where royalty once slept—if you can afford the insurance.

Air Shows on Shambok

Shambok has these fantastic air shows. With its training school for pilots famous throughout the galaxy, there is a show almost every week. How can I describe Shambokkian air shows? They're part thrilling race, part performance art, and part dance recital. Several top Shambokkian composers write music just for air shows. And some of its best artists contribute special effects, such as turning the entire sky and everything in it a dreamy golden color.

Visit to a Robot Factory

On my home planet, Dasu, the city of Nonesuch has the best robot factory in the galaxy. You can see the factory's regular operations from behind a mile-long maze of one-way mirrors. Or you can buy a ticket for the NewNew Room, where the demonstrations will amaze you. And you might split your sides laughing. That's right: Robot entertainment.

Maybe singing, dancing, and joke-telling robots aren't exactly your thing. Instead you can go to the SelfServ, where you can simulate the experience of *being* a robot *putting together* a robot.

How Can You Get Around?

Some of the planets in the Republic are pretty far from one another, so you have to take an InterPlan to travel between them. You can get anywhere within the Republic in just under eight hours. All the major cities have InterPlan ports.

On Mengrath, which is most like your Earth, you will recognize many vehicles similar to your cars, trams or trolleys, and trains. Some of the differences, however, are amazing. Trams and trains may travel on tracks 1,000 feet in the air to avoid crowding the lower levels. High, ultra-rapid elevators take you up and down.

You must have a hovercraft to travel around Torper's rain forests, Shivik's glaciers, and Krugor's thick forests. They're fun to run and crashproof, so you can drive one when you're twelve.

Who Lives in the Republic?

We're all aliens to you, but in the Tri-Star Republic we've had to learn to ignore different appearances. On Earth people differ from one another only by height, weight, the shape of certain features, and the color of their skin. You aren't used to seeing ambassadors from other solar systems and galaxies, except maybe on the video screen.

On the other hand, in the Republic, because of differences in our three solar systems and inhabited planets, intelligent life comes in many different forms. And I'm not talking here about our robots. Forms—as we call intelligent life in the Republic—come in many shapes and sizes.

On Mengrath, Forms most closely resemble people on Earth in many varieties. On the other hand, Arboreon Forms have fur, scales, fins, horns, tails, and other parts that will make you think of your Earth "animals." If you're not sure what is and what isn't a Form, just remember this simple rule: Animals are not allowed to wear clothing.

Robots

I hope I haven't made you think that you must go to the Robot Factory to see robots. In fact, on nearly every planet robots are as common as Forms, if not more so. Robots do every type of work that would be too hard or dangerous for Forms, from fixing high-voltage electrical equipment to building walls keeping giant beasts from overrunning Krugor and Torper.

Most robots work on voice commands. Of course, the most advanced robots can think for themselves and vote as citizens in our democratic elections.

Beasts

The dragons of Arboreon are huge but gentle creatures. They love to play fight. If you visit Arboreon, you will want to attend a Dragon Match, which is like one of your karate exhibitions on Earth.

The most violent beasts live on Krugor, with Torper a runner-up. Aside from those giant bees, you want to avoid the KingClaws, which are huge insectlike creatures. They have little intelligence but sharp claws and jaws. Torper's creatures are shy and generally like to avoid face-to-face meetings with Forms. But you never know if one may be in a bad mood or especially hungry. So it's best to stay inside your hovercraft and take pictures through the glass with your telephoto lens.

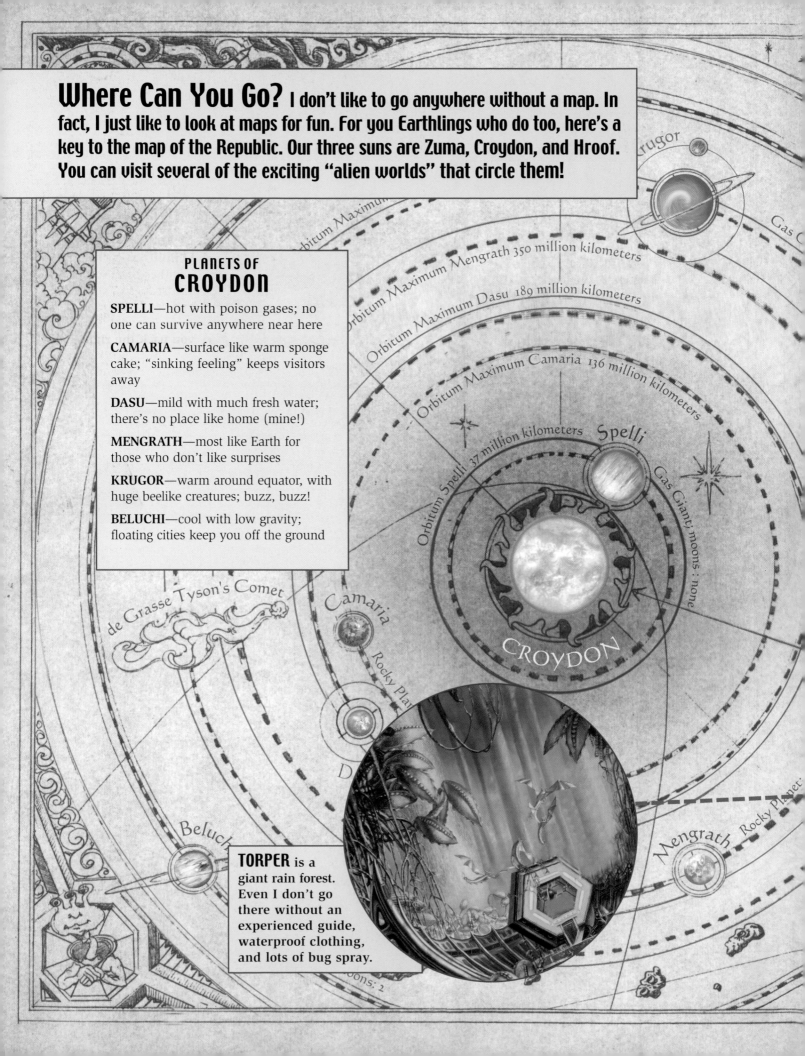

Where Can You Go?

I don't like to go anywhere without a map. In fact, I just like to look at maps for fun. For you Earthlings who do too, here's a key to the map of the Republic. Our three suns are Zuma, Croydon, and Hroof. You can visit several of the exciting "alien worlds" that circle them!

PLANETS OF
CROYDON

SPELLI—hot with poison gases; no one can survive anywhere near here

CAMARIA—surface like warm sponge cake; "sinking feeling" keeps visitors away

DASU—mild with much fresh water; there's no place like home (mine!)

MENGRATH—most like Earth for those who don't like surprises

KRUGOR—warm around equator, with huge beelike creatures; buzz, buzz!

BELUCHI—cool with low gravity; floating cities keep you off the ground

TORPER is a giant rain forest. Even I don't go there without an experienced guide, waterproof clothing, and lots of bug spray.

Orbitum Maximum Mengrath 350 million kilometers

Orbitum Maximum Dasu 189 million kilometers

Orbitum Maximum Camaria 136 million kilometers

Orbitum Spelli 37 million kilometers

Spelli

Gas Giant; moons : none

CROYDON

de Grasse Tyson's Comet

Camaria

Rocky Pla

Beluch

Mengrath

Rocky Planet

ANDROMEDA GALAXY

PLANETS OF
HROOF

GISH—poisonous gases; even the most curious stay away

LEMBAK-KROKUR—desert and mountains are OK for short visits; great scenery

SHAMBOK—like futuristic Earth; for those who love talking animals

Lembak-Krokur

HROOF

Gish

Shambok

Arboreon

Shivik

LEMBAK-KROKUR
has these strange landscapes of stone and sand. No one lives there. But if you pack the right gear, you can camp out for a few days.

number of moons: 6

moons: 12

Krokur 178 mill...

Orbitum O...

Number of moons: 2

...million kilometers) moons: 1

...of moons: 1

SHIVIK
The jagged rocks and mountains of Shivik are covered with ice and snow. Flying over its huge glaciers inside a toasty space capsule makes a great day trip.

PLANETS OF
ZUMA

PLOPLOPLOP—hot, bubbly soup; no one can live or even set foot here

TORPER—steamy rain forest; lovely place if you like hot, wet weather

ARBOREON—mild with many forests and a few cities, cold at poles; nice

SHIVIK—very cold, covered with ice and snow; bring extra blankets

In orbit around Gas Giant; Orbitum Maximum Arboreon 216 million kil...

Orbitum Max...

Orbitum M...

Torper

moons: 4

Ploploplop

moons: none

DONATO 2002

ZUMA

Help and Farewell

I've left an important point for last. If you visit the Republic and ever need help, the Galactic Positioning System (GPS) found within your SimTrans can indicate your location anywhere in the galaxy. Just speak a message into it, telling what the problem is. Are you lost? Hurt? Hungry? Quick help is on the way!

Have you enjoyed my little guidebook? I haven't had room to tell you everything, but I hope I got you interested in visiting. You can get longer guidebooks in your library or bookstore, and there are several excellent HoloVids. It helps to plan your trip, but you do want to leave some wiggle room in case there's something you're simply *wagwag* over and want to extend that part of your stay.

Farewell for now.

Astron, your friendly guide to the Republic